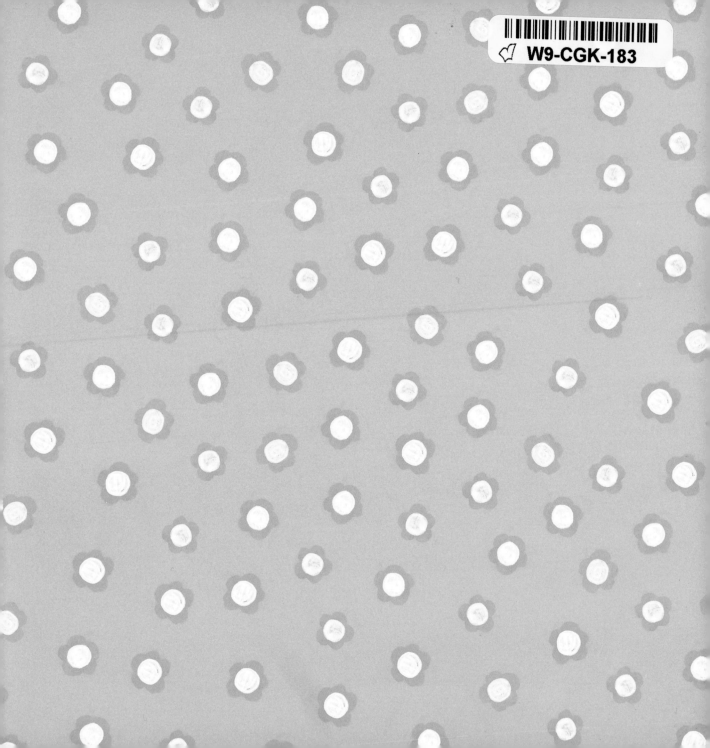

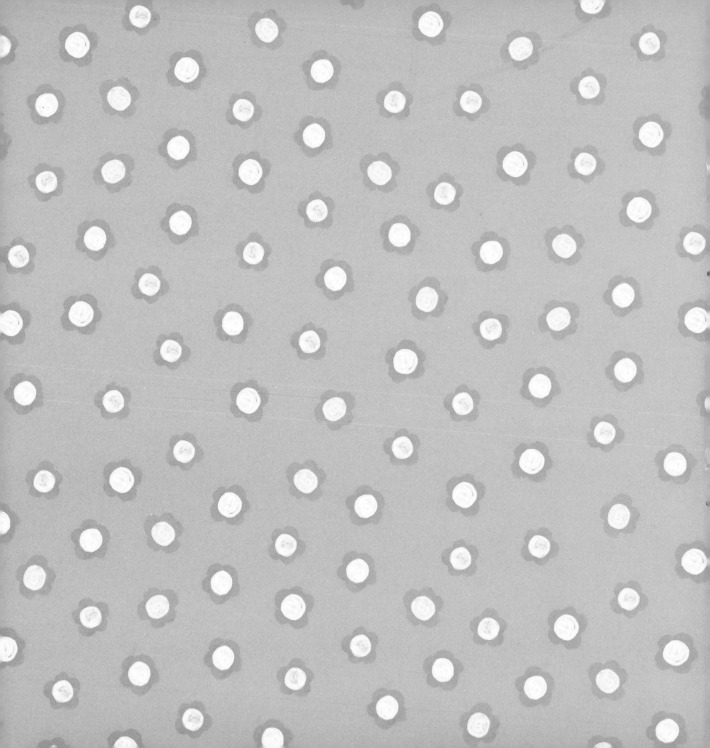

I Can Say Please

For my gorgeous daughters, Olympia and Tilly,
who have lovely manners ~T.A.

First American Edition 2011
Kane Miller, A Division of EDC Publishing

Text and illustrations copyright © 2010 Tamsin Ainslie
First published in Australia by Little Hare Books
First published in the United States of America by Kane Miller in 2011
by arrangement with Australian Licensing Corporation

Library of Congress Control Number: 2010941085

Printed through Phoenix Offset
Printed in Shen Zhen, Guangdong Province, China, April 2011
1 2 3 4 5 6 7 8 9 10
ISBN: 978-1-61067-037-1

I Can Say Please

Tamsin Ainslie

Kane Miller
A DIVISION OF EDC PUBLISHING

Let's go on a picnic!

Yes, please!

Would you like to stop here?

Yes, please!

Do you need any help?

Shall we eat now?

Yes, please!

Would you like a sandwich?

Yes, please!

Do you want
to paddle?

Yes, please!

Would you like to hold my hand?

Yes, please!

14

Shall we eat the cupcakes?

Yes, please!

Do you want to go home now?

Let's go on another picnic soon!

Yes, please!

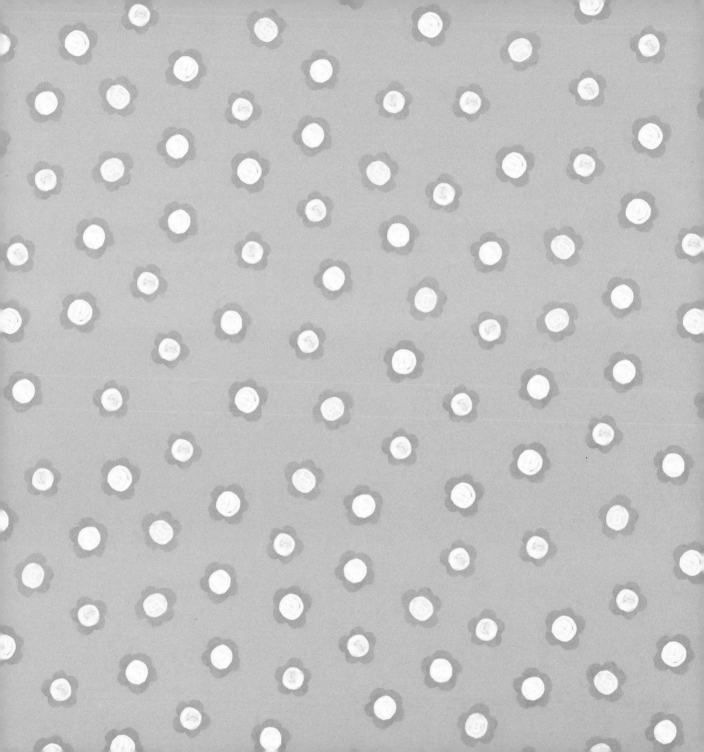